Sparkle town fairies

Esme
the
Emerald
fairy

and the Search for the Sparkle Stone

Sarah Creese * Lara Ede

make
believe
ideas

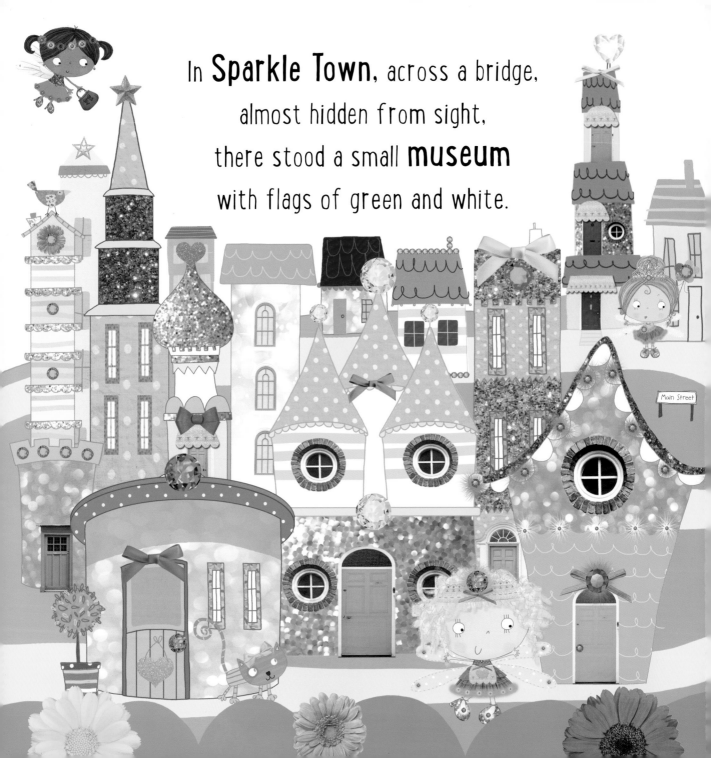

In **Sparkle Town**, across a bridge,
almost hidden from sight,
there stood a small **museum**
with flags of green and white.

This book belongs to

....

Museum

The museum kept all kinds of things,
from **books** to **giant bones**,
but best and most amazing were
its sparkling, precious **stones**.

Ooooh!

Fairy-Rex

Esme the **Emerald Fairy**
took care of each display,
making sure her fairy guests
saw something **new** each day.

With one swish of her **emerald wand,** she made each gem shine **bright.**

But because Esme
was very **shy**,
she did this
out of sight!

Esme **polished** every day,
but the fairies did not know,

The amber stones
are amazing.

for she did all this in **secret**,
too **shy** to let it show.

These are the sparkliest gems in town!

One morning, like each day before,
Esme **began** to work.

But when she waved her wand, it **FIZZED** . . .

and **POPPED** . . .

then went **BERSERK!**

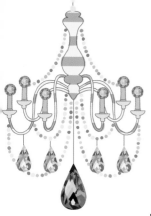

Without her wand, the sparkly stones
became so **dull** and **plain**
that the guests felt disappointed
and they started to **complain!**

Oh, dear!
These gems are *sooo* dull!

Well, I'm not
coming here again.

Seeing their friend
looking sad and blue
the fairies came to help.

We can get
this place sparkling
in no time.

But **as** they cleaned,
Susie **SNEEZED**,
and knocked a book from the shelf!

Achoo-oops!

THE MYSTERY OF THE SPARKLE STONE

The Sparkle Stone is the brightest gemstone in Fairy Land. It has not been seen for hundreds of years...

The Sparkle Stone will save the day!

Said Esme,
"Even with this book,
I'd **never** find the stone."

Daphne cried,
"We'll help you try —
you won't be on your own!"

As Esme felt uncertain still,
Susie took the lead.

And off they **flew** across the town toward the **Silver Sea**.

At last they saw a mountaintop
covered in shimmering white.
"The stone is near here," Esme said,
"that's why it's all **so bright!**"

With goggles on to shield their eyes
from all the dazzling snow,
the fairies **searched** from left to right,
then up and down below . . .

They flew along a tunnel,
then saw, carved on a wall:

Ooh, what is this?

ONLY THOSE WITH INNER LIGHT
MAY REACH THE SPARKLE HALL.

Each fairy gave the wall a tap,
but Esme felt too shy.
So the others, very gently,
encouraged her to try.

You can do it, Esme!

Esme thought of her **museum,**
and what she had to save.
She took a breath, then tapped the wall,
"Esme," she said, **"BE BRAVE."**

The wall went **crrrRUNCH,**
then cracked apart.
Esme squeezed inside.
But in a **flash,**
it all turned black!
And she was **TERRIFIED!**

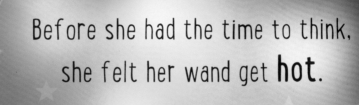

Before she had the time to think,
she felt her wand get **hot**.

It **SHOOK**

and **SHUDDERED**

and **SHIVERED**,

...then from her hand, it **shot!**

It whizzed into the darkness,
and into the unknown ...

'til suddenly the wand lit up **beneath** the SPARKLE STONE!

The stone's bright light shone all around.
Esme stared **wide-eyed**:
a narrow path stretched toward the stone,
with big **DROPS** on each side.

Her wings were **trembling** at the sight.
"I'll have to walk," she said.
Bravely she stepped onto the path,
while looking straight ahead.

With each new step, her **courage** grew,
and soon she reached the end.
She **boldly** took the stone and wand
and rushed back to her friends.

You did it, Esme!

Yippee!

Sleepily, but full of glee,
the fairies headed home.
And proudly Esme put in place
the wondrous **SPARKLE STONE.**

Wow!

Soon the museum was full again,
but **better** still than that,
was Esme's newfound **confidence**,
which brought her powers back!

What a super sight!

Now Esme's not afraid to show
just what **she can do**.

She **sparkles** on the outside –
and on the **inside**, too!